Danger for Old Ruff

Vesta J. Seek

Illustrated by
Deborah G. Wilson

Chariot Books™
David C. Cook Publishing Co.

To the memory of my mother,
who is the "Janie" in the stories.

Thank you, Pat Habada and Mel Niswander, for your
encouragement and valuable suggestions.
V.S.

For Brahm, who loves dogs, turtles, and even snakes.
D.W.

Chariot Books™ is an imprint of Chariot Family Publishing
Cook Communications Ministries, Elgin, Illinois 60120
Cook Communications Ministries, Paris, Ontario
Kingsway Communications, Eastbourne, England

DANGER FOR OLD RUFF
©1991 by Vesta Seek for text and Deborah G. Wilson for illustrations

Designed by Donna Kae Nelson
First Printing, 1991
Printed in Singapore
95 94   5 4

Library of Congress Cataloging-in-Publication Data
Seek, Vesta
        Danger for Old Ruff/ Vesta Seek: illustrated by Deborah
Wilson.
            p.   cm. — (On my own books)
        Summary: The whole family saddens when their beloved dog is
bitten by a rattle snake and becomes very ill; but, through God's good-
ness, Ruff knows how to heal himself.
        ISBN 1-55513-360-6
        I. Wilson, Deborah G., ill. II. Title. III. Series: On my own
books (Elgin, Ill.)
        [DNLM: 1. Dogs--Fiction.]
PZ7.S4516Dan   1990
[E]--dc20   89-25240
                                                                CIP

Old Ruff was a big white dog
with black spots.
He lived on a farm with Janie
and her mother and father.
Horses, cows, and chickens
were on the farm, too.

Janie called her mother "Ma."

She called her father "Pa."

Janie had three brothers.

But they were too big

to play with her much.

So Janie played with Old Ruff.

Janie loved Old Ruff.

Sometimes they would run and run.

Sometimes they would sit on the porch
and watch the birds.

Sometimes they would lie on the grass
and look at the fluffy clouds.

One morning Janie's big brothers

went to work with Pa in the field.

Ma was at work in the house.

Janie saw the chickens go to an old log.

She saw them walk in a funny way.

They looked in a hole in the log.

Then they jumped away.

They looked and jumped,

looked and jumped.

Janie called to Ma.

"Come here, Ma," she said.

"Look at the chickens.

Is something in that log?"

Ma came out to look.

"Oh, my," she said.

"I think a rattlesnake is in that log.

No! No! Ruff, stay away!

Don't go near the log!"

But Old Ruff ran to the log.

He put his nose in the hole.

And he got the rattlesnake!

He held it up high.

But the rattlesnake bit Old Ruff

on the end of his nose.

Then Old Ruff shook the rattlesnake.

He shook it and shook it.

And he killed it.

Old Ruff looked at Janie.

He wanted to say, "I did

something good.

See, I killed the rattlesnake."

But Old Ruff could not talk.

And his nose was so sore.

He did not feel good.

Janie and Ma looked at Ruff's nose.

"Oh, Ma," said Janie.

"Is Old Ruff sick?

Will Old Ruff die?

I don't want him to die."

"Maybe we can find something

to help Old Ruff," Ma said.

They went into the house

to look for something.

When they came out,

they could not see Old Ruff.

Where was he?

"Come, Ruff," called Ma.

"Here, Ruff," called Janie.

They called and called.

But Ruff did not come.

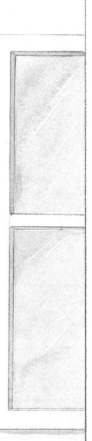

"Oh, Ma," said Janie.

"Where did Ruff go?"

"Oh, dear," said Ma.

"I think Old Ruff

went away to die.

He did not want us

to see him die."

Janie cried and cried,

and Ma cried a little, too.

When Ma went in the house to get dinner,

Janie sat on the porch.

She was very sad.

Then she talked to God.

"Dear, God," she said,

"I love Old Ruff so much.

I don't want him to die."

Soon Janie saw Pa and her big brothers
coming in from the field.

Maybe Pa can find Old Ruff, thought Janie.

She ran to Pa and told him

about Old Ruff and the rattlesnake.

Pa loved Janie so much.

It made him sad to see her cry.

"I will try to help you," he said.

Pa and the brothers

looked and looked.

They called and called.

But they could not find Old Ruff.

Janie did not want to eat.

She did not want to play.

She could only think about Old Ruff.

That night Pa held Janie on his lap.

He held her for a long time.

He did not like to see his little girl so sad.

Three days went by.

Every day Janie looked for Old Ruff.

Every day she called and called.

Every day she cried a little.

She wanted to see Old Ruff.

Oh, how she wanted to see him!

Then one day Janie saw
something very big and fat
come out of the woods.
It was white with black spots.
But it could not be Old Ruff!

Ruff was big, but he was not that big!

He was not fat like that.

The big, fat animal came slowly,

so very slowly.

Janie said, "Can this be Old Ruff?"

She looked and looked

at this big fat animal.

Then she knew.

Yes, it was Old Ruff.

"Oh, Ma, come here. Come here!"

called Janie.

"Old Ruff is home.

He is home, but look at him!

Why is he like this?"

"Poor Old Ruff," said Ma.

"He is so sick.

That rattlesnake did this to him."

Janie was happy to see Old Ruff,

but she was sad to see him like this.

Ma put some milk in a dish.

"Here, Ruff," Ma said.

"Here is some milk for you."

Old Ruff wanted to drink the milk,

but he could drink only a little.

Then he got up and walked slowly away.

He walked very, very slowly.

Ma and Janie went with Old Ruff.

"We will not let him get away

from us this time," said Ma.

"We will see where Old Ruff is going."

"Oh, yes," said Janie.

"We can't let him get away

from us this time!"

Ruff walked very slowly
into the woods.
Ma and Janie went, too.
Old Ruff walked to a stream
of water and lay down.
He let the cool water
run over him.
He put his nose in the
soft mud.
He lay very still.

In the cool water Ruff was not so hot.

The soft mud was good for his nose.

All day, Old Ruff lay there.

All night he lay there

in the cool stream of water.

All day and all night

his nose was in the soft mud.

He lay there for many days

Every day Janie went to see him.

Soon Old Ruff was not so big and fat.

He was not so hot.

Soon his nose was not so red.

Soon he wanted something to eat.

Then one day Old Ruff came home.

He could run and jump.

He could play with Janie.

"Oh, I am so happy, Ruff," said Janie.

"I am so happy that you knew what to do.

You made yourself well.

How did you know mud would

help your nose?

How did you know cool water

would be good for you?"

Ma came out to see Old Ruff.

She was happy to see him well.

"Ma," asked Janie, "how did he know

what to do?

Do you think God told him what to do?"

"God loves all the animals," said Ma.

"God loves Old Ruff.

Yes, I think God told him what to do."

That night when Pa came home

from the field

Old Ruff lay on the porch.

What a happy night it was.

"God is so good," said Janie.

"Yes," Pa said. "We want to thank God."

All the family thanked God.

Janie said, "Thank You for Old Ruff.

I love You, God. Good night."